Metamorfose

Gordon T. Alston

Published by Big G Books

Cover Illustration by Nayani Gannile based on an original sketch by the author.

Printed in the United States of America

ISBN: 978-1-7332186-8-9

For Nicole, who was as excited and interested in this story as I. Thanks for the encouragement.

ACKNOWLEDGMENTS

Much thanks to Joseph S. Kennedy for his contribution to one of the Petersburg, VA 1965 chapters. Your contribution helped me move the story in a good direction.

Metamorfose

Metamorfose

1 CHAPTER

PRESENT DAY: WHAT THE...?

I'm driving down Snowden River Pkwy when I see what appears to be a tornado come out of nowhere, heading straight for me. In my mind I'm thinking *tornado...hurricane*, *what's the difference between the two? Was it my imagination, or did it have a face?* I've seen clouds that looked like animals, angels, and other things, even Groucho Marx, but nothing like this. The face looked sinister with menacing eyes, an open laughing mouth showing sharply pointed teeth, and one of those pointy devil beards. Then, it seemed to morph into the face of a bear with the menacing eyes and a laughing fang-filled mouth. Next the face morphed into that of an eagle, with the same menacing eyes laughing mouth and a sharp beak. As the wind swirled, the faces continued to morph between one another, but never turned from looking at me.

Imagination running away or not, the one thing I knew for sure was that the tornado was huge and coming straight for me. I immediately think bank a hard left to get out of its path, but I can't judge its width, and so I settle on a full U-turn to try to outrun it. I thought if I could just get my speed up to 75 mph, I could outrun it. The only reason I picked 75 was because I thought I'd heard somewhere that that's the speed the wind needs to be to be considered a tornado or hurricane. Needless to say, I had no solid science behind this thought and wasn't even sure I had my facts right. Was the 75 mph the speed of the rotation or the speed it was moving along its tract? What's more, the wind speed could have been a lot faster. Nonetheless, 75 mph is what I thought I could reach given the situation, and so I clung to that notion the way people cling to the notion that good will triumph over evil, not because it will, but because it must. Because if we don't believe we can

Metamorfose

win, then why even try? So, I sped in the opposite direction up Snowden River Pkwy with one eye on the speedometer, one eye on the road ahead, and one eye on the tornado in my rearview mirror. I know what you are thinking, that's three eyes, and I tell you I'm not sure how many eyes I had, but I was watching everything!

As I raced for my life up Snowden River Pkwy, the thought of trying to turn out of the tornado's path kept popping into my mind, but as I swerved left the tornado seemed to swerve left, and as I swerved right it seemed to follow me that way too. Then I thought, *what did I do wrong to have God send a tornado after me?* As I raced up the road, jumbled thoughts raced through my mind, *who have I wronged, what did I do to deserve this, why me, who do I have to make amends with, when is The Day of Atonement*?

2 CHAPTER

PETERSBURG, VA 1965: GIT 'N DA HOUSE

It is the most terrifying sound you'll hear in your life. I don't know if it sounds like a freight train. I do know it sounds like death. I grabbed my great-grandfather's work-gnarled hand.

"Granddad, do you hear that? "I asked with widened eyes. My heart was racing and so were my words.

At first, he didn't answer me, he was somewhere else, in the distance – his eyes reliving past horrors.

I shook his hand, as if trying to wake him from a deep sleep and asked, no shouted, again with rising fear in

Metamorfose

my young voice, "granddad, do you hear that!

"Slowly coming back to the present, in a surprisingly calm voice close to a whisper, but still with a far-off look in his eyes he said, "Yes. Boy I need ya ta git 'n da house. Tell momma to git errbody ta da basement."

I shouted, "What is it Granddad? What is it?"

"Marcus, I dun told yah ta git goin' boy," he said while motioning his finger toward the house.

I took off in a full run from my grandfather's garden, where I'd been helping him pull weeds and inspect the many plantings. At my age, the garden was like a mini farm. It was about fifty yards from my great-grandfather's house and had a fence around it made of rusting chicken wire and wooden posts that looked to be seven feet high. He always kept its gate locked so us kids wouldn't be tempted to go in the garden alone. The length and width of the garden must have been 20 to 30 yards each, and almost every inch of the plot had something growing on it. There were tomato plants, watermelon vines, cucumber vines, string beans, cabbage, and who knows what else. I was fond of the tomatoes and watermelon, so I didn't pay much attention to the other plants. I remember saying one day that I was going to climb the fence and eat up all the watermelons, at which point my mother reminded me, as she and every other grownup had done to all my brothers, sisters, and cousins, that there were also snakes in the garden. My grandfather always carried his hoe with him while he was in the garden, in case he needed it to cut the head off any snake he came across.

I made it across the fifty-yard expanse and turned the corner around the little backyard where my grandfather also kept a few chickens, all the while yelling "Mama, grandad said to get everyone in the basement." I bounded up the two steps to the weather-worn wooden back porch and yanked open the back screen door, with its aged chipping paint and rusted screens, still repeating "Mama, grandad said to get everyone in the basement."

It was clear my mother and everyone else had heard that awful freight train sound because by the time I reached her, she had already begun herding everyone into the basement, and was turning off whatever was cooking on the stove and any lights that were on in the house. This was actually our drill for every storm no matter its expected severity. We'd turn off all the lights, and stove if someone was cooking, take candles and the radio to the basement, and sit quietly in the candlelight until the storm was over.

3 CHAPTER

PRESENT DAY: THE QUARINITY

I tried to steady the car. I was doing close to 90 mph now and still the tornado was gaining on me. The winds whipped my car, rocking it from side to side, with a roaring laughter getting ever closer to me. I gripped the steering wheel as tight as I could to keep from losing control of the car. Out of desperation, I took one hand off the steering wheel. Forcing my still clinched fingers open, I pressed the blue button on my rear-view mirror.

"OnStar. How can I help you Mr. Elstone?", a voice said.

I thought to myself, *how do you tell someone a tornado is about to kill you? How do you tell them it has three*

Metamorfose

changing faces that are scarier than any movie you have ever seen, and that the faces are laughing at your attempt to escape them?

"Mr. Elstone, are you still there? We have been informed that there is abnormal weather in your area."

"It's a tornado," I yelled.

"OnStar is not equipped to deal with tornados, the voice said; I will connect you to the National Oceanic Atmospheric Administration."

"No, don't connect me to NOAA. I know those guys, they won't help me, it's a long story. I've got a different request; can you tell me someone I need to make amends with?"

"Oh, that list is pretty long" the OnStar voice replied. "Should I start with the A's and go forward or the Z's and go backward?" *If I had a fourth eye, I would have rolled it.*

"Just start randomly and give me the first name that comes up," I said.

Metamorfose

The OnStar voice said "James Bullings."

I asked, "Who the heck is James Bullings?"

"He is the sight-impaired gentleman that you laughed at when you saw him run into the directory pole in the subway when he was running to catch the train," OnStar replied.

"I didn't really laugh," I said. "It was a stifled laugh, and I still have the marks from where I bit my lip holding it in. Besides, I picked up the thick lens that popped out of his eyeglasses and helped him put it back in the frame and helped him catch the next train."

The OnStar voice said, "I just give you the information I'm provided with."

I thought to myself, *I'm glad OnStar also ends sentences with prepositions.*

I continued to speed ahead, pushing 90 mph, trying to elude the tornado, all the while trying to reason with an anonymous OnStar voice that had way too much information about me. As the tornado gained on me, I yelled, maybe to OnStar, maybe to God, maybe to both,

Metamorfose

"Okay, I will go find Mr. Bullings!" Within minutes the tornado disappeared just as quickly as it had appeared, and I thought *could God be more than the Trinity? Could He be the Quarinity; the Father, Son, Holy Ghost, and OnStar?*

4 CHAPTER

PETERSBURG, VA 1965: SPARED

I was scared to death as we sat in the southwest corner of the almost pitch-black basement, lit only with one barely flickering candle held by my mother. Considering the number of us gathered in the basement, being in the southwest corner meant being as close to the southwest corner as 25 people could get. The Fisher household included Pop Fisher, his daughters Willie and Lauri, Willie's daughter Gail with her husband and seven kids, and Lauri's husband and their twelve kids. The younger kids always called Pop Fisher grandad although he was their great-grandfather, everyone else in the house mostly called him Pop.

Metamorfose

Even in the basement we could hear the awful chugging sound of the tornado.

"I'm scared mamma," I said with a tremble in my voice.

"Hysh" my mother said, with the dim flicker of a candle only illuminating her face, giving her an eerie bodyless appearance.

If it wasn't for the fact that it was my mother's face that had comforted me through so many scrapes and sicknesses, I would have been even more terrified.

My grandfather who had been rocking back and forth mumbling something of a prayer broke his trance for a second and said, "boy yah bet be quiet while da Lawd dus his werk." As his voice trailed off, he added, "da Lawd werks n sterious ways," then he went back to his incantations.

We could hear the windows begin to rattle as the chugging roar came closer. We huddled closer together, my grandfather still off to himself rocking and murmuring his prayers. The frame of the house began to creek as it tried to stand its ground against the violent wind whips. Pressing ourselves into the corner as far as we could fit, my mother quietly hummed "We Shall Not Be Moved." Although she wasn't singing the lyrics, I pictured the imagery of the song in my head- *a palm tree standing by a river, being blown so hard that it was almost horizontal to the ground, its big palm leaves flapping and being torn and ripped, but its roots still grounded in the bank of the river, holding on for dear life.*

When the tornado had passed, I felt a relief I couldn't explain. Yes, I was relieved that the worst had passed, and that the basement we huddled in was still intact, but somewhere deep down in my mind or spirit I felt a different type of calm flowing through me.

We emerged from the basement not knowing what to expect. I pictured the rest of the house missing; with broken off pipes, fragments of wooden walls, and the remains of a staircase. As we each filed out, we looked around in amazement at how little damage there was. There were broken windows and some picture frames off the wall. The dining room tablecloth was jumbled at one end of the table, being saved from hitting the floor only by the chair that sat at the head of the table. There were also various papers strewn about, but all-in-all, things weren't in as bad a shape as I had imagined. I wish I could say the same thing for our neighbors' houses. As we walked out onto our front porch, we could see piles of rubble, up and down the road, where houses used to stand. The picture I had of what I expected our house to look like was what I was now seeing. Some houses were missing their top floors, others were missing everything down to the ground. Fences were ripped up and wrapped around whatever had stopped them from blowing completely away. Some cars were moved from where they had been last parked, while others were flipped upside-down or on to their sides. The view was the same from our back porch. The tornado had done a great deal of damage to almost every house as far as I could see but seemed to spare ours.

5 CHAPTER

PRESENT DAY: FINDING A BULLINGS IN A CHINA SHOP

Making my way back down Snowden River Pkwy, with the thought of trying to locate James Bullings, a blind man that the anonymous voice told me was first on my list, a guy I barely met 30 years ago as he ran for a subway train- *what blind man runs for a train?* - I felt a relief I couldn't explain.

I flipped my starting point over and over in my mind and of course thought, *The Yellow Pages.* I had always called all phone books the Yellow Pages, the way some people call all sodas Coke. What I really meant was the White Pages since I was looking for a person and not a business. I started with the Washington DC White Pages since I had seen him at the Federal Triangle Metro Station. I only found listings for the name James Bolling and derivatives of that name, like James Bolling Jr., etc. Next, I searched the other surrounding Maryland and Virginia county White Pages, since the Metro, with its tendrils reaching out from its primary wheel and spoke structure that encircled DC proper, ferried in people from the entire Washington Metropolitan Area. The Metro not only reached to the counties bordering DC but went to some of the counties just past those counties.

It took me a couple of weeks, but I finally located James Bullings by using Google Search. I probably would have saved myself a lot of time if I'd started with Google, but my old-school brain had dialed up the White Pages first, so that's where I started. To my surprise James Bullings was closer than I would have imagined. The search site gave the address of what turned out to be a store located in historic Ellicott City. Ellicott City is the sister city of Columbia, where I had moved to just a few years ago. Columbia is the "new" city, having only been

Metamorfose

founded 1967; whereas, Ellicott City, although it has new development, is old and the historic area dates back to before the founding of the country. I've never liked historic parts of cities; if you watch any movie nothing good ever happens in the old parts of the cities. For me, you may as well replace "historic" with "creepy. I wished I had Googled some information about the city before I left, but I've never been that enamored with technology. Heck, I just started using Facebook to reconnect with Junior High School friends the past summer, years after my friends were already on it. I didn't use GPS for directions either. Me and my old-school brain just headed North on Route 29 to US 40, then looked for the signs.

To get to Historic Ellicott City, I followed signs which led me to a road that snaked downward into what in the old days would have been called a valley. Come to think of it; it might still be called a valley today. I drove past old buildings that had been transformed into new eclectic businesses. There was a building with and old "Hardware" sign that now sold knick-knacks and newer kitchen accessories, and another one that, judging by

Metamorfose

the smell in the air, now probably functioned as a coffee house. At the bottom of the road was an elevated railroad trestle, and behind it was an old B&O Railroad building; I wondered if it was the railroad museum someone had mentioned to me back when I first moved to Columbia.

I swung my car around and made my way a little ways back up the road as I looked for a parking spot. I parked in front of a building with a large picture window that now hosted small weddings; there was actually a wedding going on inside; must have been about 10 people in all including the bride and groom. After getting out of the car I headed for the coffee house, although I don't drink coffee, I figured a shot of caffeine would help justify the wired angst I was feeling. The coffee house turned out to be more than just a coffee house; it had baked goods, an ample vegan menu, and a breakfast menu that included bacon. Like the other stores, this mix of vegan and bacon fit the city. There was a mix of patrons inside; hippy-type old couples with long greying hair flowing over multicolored tops; young bohemians on their laptops, probably writing a screenplay or 'the next great novel'; tourist types looking around at everything and everybody as if they've never seen a business or its patrons before. The regulars probably put me in this category.

As I waited for my coffee, I spotted the men's room and thought *I'd better empty my bladder just to be safe*. The last thing I wanted was to have to use the bathroom at a critical moment. While in the men's room I heard a rumbling sound. As I tried to determine the source of the sound my heart began to race; *was it a train*? This would make sense, since the railroad was only a few yards away. I wondered if the railroad was functional.

"Please let it be a train," I silently begged.

Was it a tornado?

In all out fear, I ran from the bathroom, sweat pouring down my face. To my surprise, no one else had moved or even looked up. The girl behind the counter just stared at me as she handed me my coffee. I left the coffee house feeling a little out of sorts.

I started to walk up the street looking for the address I

Metamorfose

found for Mr. Bullings. As I passed a small footbridge nestled between two buildings, I noticed that there was a large creek running under the bridge, and also under most of the buildings. Each building sat on two huge steel beams that spanned the banks of the creek. The beams were the kind that were in that picture of construction workers eating lunch while sitting on a beam suspended high above an emerging skyscraper. My eyes lingered on the sight of water running right under the buildings as I wondered if the buildings were originally built on the beams or if the beans were wedged under the buildings as the erosive water cut a path under them over many years. This explained the rumbling sound I heard in the men's room, and better explained a light musty smell that permeated the coffee house.

As I walked up the street, I figured a residence amongst the businesses would stick out like... *like a Bullings in a China shop,* I thought to myself, then laughed audibly at my own joke. However, all the buildings had been converted to businesses, at least their first floors had been.

Metamorfose

Making my way pass each store's windows reminded me of window-shopping with my mother as a child. When we didn't have money to spend, my mother would take us window-shopping. We would spend hours walking around downtown Washington DC marveling at the store displays. If we were lucky, a few of the items we saw would end up as birthday or Christmas presents. Passing each store, I promised myself that I'd come back with my wife and kids not only to window-shop, but to maybe buy a few things.

As I browsed from one store to the next, I came to the address I had found for James Bullings; it was a store that sold Native American artifacts and chocolate. I slowly walked in like any other customer and began to peruse their merchandise. Some of the artifacts looked authentic, some items looked like you could get them at any gift shop. There were drum skins, turquoise jewelry, dream catchers, pecan caramel clusters, fudge, chocolate covered pretzels, and many other trinkets and goodies. There were two people running the store. One was a tall guy who looked to be in his late forties or early fifties. Greying hair reached his shoulders, framing

Metamorfose

the fine features of his clean-shaven face. He wore what looked like a grey hand-sewn deer skin vest over a beige, cotton, long sleeved shirt, and black khakis. The vest's outline was rough-cut, its sides loosely stitched together with leather lacing that wove around in a spiral down the sides, with about an inch between each looping, and tied at the bottom of the vest. It had four silver buttons, about the size of nickels, each with two small slits near the middle where more leather lacing attached them to one side of the vest. On the opposite side of the vest there were four six-inch leather tassels attached to the vest. Each tassel consisted of two strands of leather lacing knotted about two inches from where they were attached, with a small white bead knotted on to each tip of the tassel. The two-inch space between the vest and the first knot was where the button fit to hold the vest closed. There was also leather fringe across each side of the vest about four inches down from where the vest rested on his shoulders. The vest looked authentic.

The other person running the store was a woman in her forties who looked like she could be deer-vest's sister, although I've heard that people who are married long enough will start to resemble each other. She had the same fine-featured face with long grey-streaked brown hair. She wore a loose-fitting cotton dress that flowed down her body, which gave the appearance of wind continually blowing it. The color of the dress was like a navy-blue canvas painted with many varieties of gold flowers accented with white. The flowers were in various groupings and patterns, in some places stealing the whole scene, in others melting away into golden spatters against a beautiful dark night. The neckline was an embroidered "Y" with a V-neck that ended with a stitched-together double stem where the two sides of the "V" met.

Deer-vest was chatting with a couple about things that seemed to be unrelated to the items in the store. Likewise, flowing-dress was speaking with what appeared to be a mother-daughter pair, again about things that seemed to be unrelated to the items in the store. I had an immediate affinity for the "perhaps" siblings who seemed to be more interested in the people that visited their store than pushing their merchandise.

They let me roam around the store without once stopping their conversations to ask if they could help me find something. In most stores the salespeople hound you to let them help you buy something and seem nervous if you are just walking around not asking questions.

I made my way back to the front of the store, where the man was having his conversation, to look at the turquoise bracelets. My wife lost the one she bought when we were in Santa Fe, and since her birthday was coming up, a new one would make a great gift. While eyeing the bracelets I could hear the conversation change to the drum skins on the wall. The man was explaining to the couple that they are made from different types of skins; some were Elk, some were cow, etc. Then he broke the conversation to tell his sister, who wasn't too far from him, that he discovered that their father still had an old, big, drum in his attic. She said she knew it was there; but he seemed surprised and amused that he had forgotten it. The couple that had been looking at the drum skins eventually left without making a purchase, and as before, the owner uninterested in engaging me in a conversation about buying something, went to straighten some items.

After looking through more of the store, I approached deer-vest and asked to see the bracelets in the case. As he pulled them out, he informed me that they were handmade by someone he knew that was part of the Navajo Nation, and that the bracelets were made of turquoise and hand-worked silver. He said that turquoise was a bringer of good fortune, and that the Navajo not only used it in jewelry but stored it in baskets or hung pieces of it from their ceilings to ward off evil from their homes. Based on his whole approach to interacting with customers, I had no reason to doubt his word. I told him about the lost bracelet, and as I described it, he began mentioning names of several different tribes that could have been the artisans that made it. Our conversation meandered to talk of the Santa Fe horizon with its colorful sunsets that provided magnificent backdrops to huge mesas. We talked about the Jemez Mountains near Los Alamos, which revealed a beautiful meadow as you reached the top of one of its summits, and we also talked about the ancient pueblos that where cut into the sides of cliffs. Our conversation eventually wound its way back to the bracelets he was showing me, and I selected one that I thought my wife would love.

After purchasing the bracelet and some chocolates, I told him that I had actually come to the store trying to find a man I had a chance encounter with about 30 years ago named Mr. James Bullings.

He said, "you mean Bull Wings," adding a pause after "Bull" and emphasis to the "W" in Wings".

I was fairly sure that both OnStar and the search site used Bullings but thinking to myself that the name was close enough, I said "yes." *My old-school brain reminded me to not put too much trust in technology.*

He said, "my father's name is James Bull Wings."

I asked if his father was sight impaired and he said "yes."

6 CHAPTER

THE 1800S: ANDREW'S CHANCE

Andrew's heart is pounding inside his chest as he silently enters the room. Three other men are already in the room seated at a table with their backs to Andrew, having a discussion and waiting for him to show up before Jackson's people arrive. A burly man with a ruddy deep creased face and a full dark beard was sitting between the other two men and was leading the conversation. The guy to his left was of average build with brown curling hair and scruffy facial hair and nodded more than he spoke. The one on the right seemed impatient and often interrupted the guy in the middle. These are men he had come to know well,

Metamorfose

working beside them for their cause. *This is my chance,* Andrew thought to himself, *when you kill the head, the body will perish.*

7 CHAPTER

PRESENT DAY: A MEETING WITH MR. BULL WINGS

I described to deer-vest the chance encounter I had with his father, and for the first time since I had been in the store, I sensed some animosity. I quickly explained that the thought of the encounter popped into my head the other day while I was driving and that I felt-searching for a good word I said- "compelled" to see him.

With his friendly temperament returning, he said, "My dad, if he remembers the incident, will be surprised you came to see him after all these years."

Metamorfose

I asked if I would be able to speak to him today, and he said that his dad lived right above the store.

As I thought about it, I figured most of the store owners must live above their stores. The buildings were huge with four or five stories, and the shops couldn't have been pulling in enough money to cover the costs of the entire building.

He told me that his father usually meditated around this time of day and suggested I come back in about two hours. He asked if it was my first visit to Ellicott City, and, me, having answered yes, he suggested I finish exploring the city. Since the store wasn't crowded, and me wanting to take advantage of the wait to learn more about the man OnStar had instructed me to see, I asked if he'd mind if I just hung around the store.

As I hung around, being the affable people, they seemed to be, he and his sister were more than happy to chat with me in between customers. I slowly paced my questions about his father, making sure to amble around the store and sprinkle in a question here and

31

there about the merchandise. I learned that James Bull Wings and his wife had started the store to give Native-American artisans a place to sell their work. It also allowed Mrs. Bull Wings to essentially be a stay-at-home mom as she raised her two young children since the family lived above the store, while James went to his full-time job in Washington DC. She would open the store at 11:30am to be ready for customers who were on their lunch breaks. Although there were one or two customers who would come in when she opened, the foot traffic would pick up just after 12 noon and would dwindle by 2:00pm. The customers were always considerate whenever Mrs. Bull Wings needed to momentarily tend to one of the children's needs. Foot traffic would begin to pick up again around 4:00pm when people were getting off from work. Since his day at the DC job started at 6:30am, James would normally get home to the store between 4:00pm and 4:30pm, in time to take over for the evening rush.

Deer-vest and his sister had grown up in this store and began helping their parents run it as soon as they were big enough, first by sweeping the floor and emptying the trash cans, then by assisting customers and ringing up purchases. Holidays and summer breaks were spent working in the store and this continued during their college breaks. After college, deer-vest took a job in Memphis, Tennessee as an auditor, while after her graduation, his sister remained in Maryland and continued to assist with the running of the store, working beside her mother during the day and her father during the evening.

She eventually took over running the store full-time when, first, her father's sight began to fail, and then her mother's health began to fail. During this time Deer-vest took a pay cut to take the job in Washington, DC to be closer to home and assist his sister and father with the store in the evenings. They explained that the store is what helped put them through college, bought the first used car they had, which got handed down to the sister when the brother went to college, and had provided for so much priceless family time together. They said it was their obligation to keep the store going, now that their mother was deceased and now that their father was older.

Metamorfose

When deer-vest said his father should be done with his
meditation by now, I was surprised at how quickly the
time had passed. He led me through the store and up a
set of steps that were situated in the far corner of a
kitchen located at the back of the store. The kitchen
was set up for making the chocolate they sold. The
stairs opened to a floor just above the store and then
continued to another floor above that one. He led me to
the floor that was two levels above the store. The steps
ended at what must have been the living room of the
top floor living quarters. The room was comfortable,
with a soft micro-fiber hunter green couch and
matching chair, and all sorts of curiosities on tables and
the walls. There was one small statue that reminded me
of Degas' "The Little Fourteen-Year-Old Dancer"
sculpture, except this woman was an adult, obese, and
unclothed. While waiting, I realized that this was the
source of the music that was quietly playing throughout
the store. All while I was in the store, I had been
unconsciously listening to the music that was being
piped in; it sounded *new-agey, spa-ish*. As I sat there, I
could hear it much clearer, and guessed that it was

Metamorfose

Native American music, maybe something from a Putumayo compilation.

When the man returned with his father, I suddenly felt embarrassed that I had never offered my name or asked him his. *For some reason I've always had a habit of assigning people names instead of just asking them their name. In Graduate School I assigned a girl the name "New Do" because she came to class with a new hairstyle that seemed to make her beam. During a discussion with some classmates one day, a classmate referred to her by name, but I couldn't put the name with the face, and when I finally figured it out, I said "oh, you mean New Do." That name stuck with her for the rest of Graduate School. There was this time when I ran into a guy I had known in Undergraduate School, who hung out with a guy I knew named Tommy. I was coming out of the subway station that he was going into, and we stopped to catch up with what we'd each been doing since school. At the end of the conversation, he said "you know, Tommy and I had a bet going that you and your buddy Joseph doesn't know my name." I looked at him with a smile and said, "Yes we do, your*

Metamorfose

name is Tommy number 2"- a name I had given him
because he was always with Tommy. He just laughed
and said they knew it, as he ran down the escalators,
without telling me his actual name. Maybe he knew
he'd always be Tommy 2 to me, even if I did finally know
his real name.

As I reflexively stretched my hand towards the father, forgetting his impairment, I said "hi, I'm Marcus Elstone."

As his father reached for my hand, embarrassed even more by my second lapse, I moved my hand about a foot to the left to meet his, and turned my head towards the son and apologized for not asking him his name. The son replied that his name was James Jr., but that most people called him Jay.

Jay helped his father, who must have been close to totally blind now, sit down, and then headed back to the store. With a voice similar to Wilfred Brimley's, Mr. Bull Wings said, "I don't get many visitors, what can I do you for?" I proceeded to tell Mr. Bull Wings about our chance encounter 30 years ago. I told him how I was rushing into the Federal Triangle Metro Station on my way home from work, as I did every weekday, and how I saw him, the only person left on the platform, run for the train. He said "So that was you in the subway that day! You laughed when I hit the pole while trying to catch the train."

Thinking *a stifled laugh* I said yes, and that I was sorry.

He said, "I'm the one who's sorry, because you may be the person that I was trying to find that day."

Perplexed, I said "huh?"

He said, "Yes, I had a vision that I was to find someone that day, and that the person would be catching the train at a certain time, and that I would bump into them while getting on the train and they would assist me to a seat and start a conversation. It was when I didn't bump into anyone that I backed off of the train and then panicked when I heard the door chime and ran to re-board the train thinking that maybe I had let them get by me. I guess I don't blame you now for laughing at the time; what blind man runs for a train?"

"A stifled laugh," I interjected, "it was a stifled laugh."

He said, "I remember being pretty angry, actually I was pissed; pissed because I felt stupid for acting on a vision that turned out to be wrong, pissed for running into the directory, and pissed because some A-hole was now laughing at my misfortune. It wasn't until, after I left the train, that it occurred to me that maybe you were the one I was to meet, but still being pissed, I said screw it, he'll get what he gets."

"Thanks," I said, with mocked sarcasm.

He said, "That's why I apologize, I shouldn't have let my anger rule my mind."

I told him that I would have normally been on that train, but that I had slipped on an icy spot just outside the subway, and after getting up I stopped by the kiosk to notify the station manager. I told the manager that I assumed that there was an air conditioning line just beneath the ground that may have malfunctioned, because I wasn't sure what else would cause an ice patch in August. After a pause I queried, "So we are even?"

"I suppose so," he replied with a chuckle.

Just when my anxiety about how my visit would be received by James Bull Wings after discovering I was the "A-hole" from the subway subsided, he said, "Now we need to find out why it was important for us to meet." Trying my best to have my voice sound rational and sane, I explained to him that I had come to find him, not based on a vision, but based on what seemed to be a tri-faced Tornado and a suggestion from OnStar.

I said, "I thought I was supposed to find you to apologize for being mildly amused at your misfortune."

He said, "That doesn't explain why I was supposed to find you in the first place.

Metamorfose

In the middle of our discussion, a song that I recognized caught my ear, and I said "hey, that's Matt Geraghty's "Metamorfose" isn't it?"

I told him how I had seen Matt perform in Chicago at a place on the Navy Pier, and how he'd given me and my wife an autographed CD; and how "Metamorfose" was my favorite song owing to the unintelligible words which were somewhat hypnotic, but which freed me to focus more on the instrumentation. *A lot of times awful lyrics ruin great instrumentation and there are a number of songs where I wish I could just erase the lyrics.*

"The words are only unintelligible to those who do not speak the language," Mr. Bull Wings said. He explained, "The song is an old Native American song that has been passed on through the years, and I was delighted when I happened to hear a new version of it one day. It's sort of a song of repentance and the lyrics loosely translate into *spare me oh Great Spirit and I will be transformed into something better, or I will transform myself and do better*. Some believe it originated with dying elders who were repenting for the wrongs or mistakes they had made in this life, and were petitioning to comeback as something better, like a deer or a buffalo. Others believe it originated as a pact between a person and the Great Spirit because the person did something they shouldn't have done or didn't do something they should have done. Kind of like when I didn't continue to try to find you."

"Well, it looks like fate, or something wanted us to meet and now that it's finally happened, let's figure out why," Mr. Bull Wings concluded.

8 CHAPTER

THE 1800S: FEET OF CLAY

Andrew stood there, with feet of clay for what felt like an eternity, shaking on the inside but trying to steady himself. He contemplated the futures that would result from his actions today, and contemplated how history would portray him, villain, or hero. He breathed deeply and moved toward the men seated at the table, rubbing a sweaty palm across his thigh toward his holster. As he got close to the man seated in the middle, Andrew raised his hand and put it on the man's shoulder and said, "I believe what we are doing here today is the right thing to do for our people, whether they realize it now or not." His feet felt fifty pounds lighter and so did his heart. "History will bare us out, he added." He had done it. He had made the jump from infiltrator to collaborator, on the way, betraying his brother John.

9 CHAPTER

THE 1800S: THE CHEROKEE NATIONAL COUNCIL

When the United States began to renege on its treaty
with the Cherokee Nation, John Acquetakey, as head of
the Cherokee National Council started advocating for
Cherokee resistance, and lobbying President John
Quincy Adams, who was an Indian sovereignty
supporter, to enforce the treaty. Things changed for the
worst when gold was discovered in Georgia, and when
Andrew Jackson, a supporter of Indian removal was
elected President. In response to this new dangerous
reality, some members of the Cherokee Nation Council
advocated for signing a new treaty the U.S.

Metamorfose

Government, under Jackson, offered, ceding all rights to their land and vacating Georgia, Alabama, Tennessee, and North Carolina in exchange for land out West and more promises.

In the Presidential election Andrew Jackson beat John Quincy Adams in a landslide victory, ensuring that no "corrupt bargain" would deny him his rightful place as President of the United States, as was done to him after he'd won a plurality but not a majority of the popular and electoral vote in the 1824 elections. In that election, with no candidates winning a majority of the votes, the election of the President was decided by a contingent election held by the United States House of Representatives, presided over by Henry Clay the Kentuckian Speaker of the House. Although Clay was one of the original candidates for the Presidency, he garnered less votes than three other candidates, including Jackson, Adams, and Secretary of the Treasury William Crawford who had suffered a severe stroke and was an invalid. Having had a long contentious rivalry with Jackson and believing that Jackson and Crawford were unsuitable for the presidency, Clay threw his support behind Adams who subsequently won the contingent election.

With Jackson's election, disagreements about what course of action the Cherokee National Council should take grew stronger. John and many members of the Council still believed strongly in demanding the enforcement of the current treaty, however, other members believed that this path of action would lead to a massacre now that Jackson was President and felt a stronger urgency to press for immediate action on signing the new treaty. As soon as John called the Council meeting to order, Bert Thompson, a burly man with a ruddy deep creased face and a full dark beard stood up without being formally recognized to speak. "John, we've gotten nowhere with Adams on honoring our treaty and now that Jackson is President, we have no chance in hell of them honoring it. Jackson is a madman and won't hesitate to take our land and slaughter us all, like he did when he went into Florida."

Andrew supported his brother's position but felt Jackson's election warranted a re-evaluation of that

position, causing Andrew to advocate for the Council to
at least consider the merits of the arguments for signing
a new treaty. With the rift on the Council growing wider
and more contentious, John met with a few trusted
allies to come up with a plan for preventing the Council
from splitting itself apart.

10 CHAPTER

THE 1800S: THE ACQUETAKEYS

John and Andrew Acquetakey grew up in one of the major clans of the Cherokee Nation. Although only eleven months separated their ages, one month their ages overlapped and they were the same age, John always seemed much older than Andrew. John had what people referred to as an "old soul." He was the serious, contemplative child. He took his role as older brother, no matter how slight, seriously and was always advising his brother Andrew on all things little and big. Andrew was more carefree and fun loving, maybe because John was always there to watch over him.

Metamorfose

Andrew looked up to John even though their father had always treated them as twins, teaching them things at the same time. They learned their chores together, how to feed the animals, how to sow seeds, how to harvest their plantings, how to fish, and how to use various tools. All along the way, John jumped in to make sure Andrew learned the chores correctly, many times before Andrew even had the chance to make mistakes. Although this irritated Andrew at times, he was quieted knowing his brother only meant the best for him. John's father would sometimes admonish John about not letting Andrew learn on his own, especially at times when John's mastery of tasks was not up to snuff. This would prompt Andrew to chime in with "See John, you are not always right," although he knew John was right most of the time.

During their teen years, it was John who secretly admired Andrew because Andrew had an openness and freeness that John struggled to reach. John would wait to be invited to join in on whatever activity the teens were doing, while Andrew would just show up and join in, even if he didn't know the other teens. He would just join in and when the fun was over, the others would ask each other "who was your friend" only to realize that no one knew him. Andrew would come back again and again until he was eventually everyone's friend. Often it was Andrew who would then invite John into the group. It's not that John meant to be standoffish, it's just that he never felt comfortable just joining in if he wasn't participating at the start and felt this way even more so if he didn't already know you. However, once John was part of it, he warmed to everyone and was just as gregarious as Andrew.

11 CHAPTER

THE 1800S: TRUSTED ALLIES

The allies John trusted most were Joe Ahaisse, Adam
Jonasse, and his brother Andrew. Joe was older than
the other men and was the previous head of the
Council. He was the one who recruited and backed John
for the position. Adam was John and Andrew's cousin
but grew up like a brother since their families lived close
to each other. While Joe was a staunch vocal supporter
of John's plan, Adam and Andrew came across as more
moderate and willing to reach a compromise, but
privately always assured John that they were one
hundred percent behind the Council's decision.

Metamorfose

Although there were many other members that backed John's position, it was these three people that he relied on to keep the Council together.

The four men met at John's house. John and his family lived in the house where he and Andrew had grown up, having moved back in after his father passed away and his mother had gotten too old to manage the house by herself. The Acquetakey house had always been a welcoming place where everyone and anyone could come and hang out ever since the brothers were kids. Their parents acted as surrogate parents to kids and adults alike, feeding them, listening to their dreams or problems, and offering advice and comfort.

As they sat in the living room, John began, "The Government is trying to divide and conquer us! We cannot let this Council tear itself apart!"

Joe added, "It was our unity that enabled us to successfully negotiate the Treaty with the Government and it will be our unity that will force them to honor it!"

Metamorfose

Addressing Adam and Andrew, John said "Because the two of you have not taken sides in the meetings, I believe you can be a strong voice for unity. Every chance you get, during individual conversations, and in the meetings, talk about the importance of standing together despite differences. Keep me abreast of people's responses and sentiments to your calls for unity, and of any other discussions.

Adam and Andrew's reports back to John were mixed. Many people, both those that supported making the Government honor the existing treaty and those that supported the signing of a new treaty, agreed that any divisions could permanently weaken the Council's ability to make the Government honor any of its promises, but there were a handful of people who believed the prevention of an imminent slaughter of the Cherokee people outweighed all else. One day Adam and Andrew reported to John that some members that advocated for signing the new treaty had begun calling themselves The Treaty Party. It was at this point that John asked Andrew to fully join the group and gain their trust so that he could gain inside knowledge of what they were discussing. Although Adam offered to be the one to join the group, John believed it was best to have his younger brother who had always looked up to him join. Andrew had always looked up to and followed John's lead even when he thought John might be wrong, and John needed this type of loyalty now.

In his private discussions with various other people Andrew made sure they got the feeling that he was beginning to doubt John's stance. In subsequent Council meetings Andrew slowly moved from his moderate stance to backing various arguments for signing a new treaty. After one particularly heated meeting Bert Thompson pulled Andrew aside and asked, "Andrew, can you please try to talk some since into John?" Andrew responded, "I have been for weeks now, and he just won't budge." As he left, Andrew promised Bert he would continue to try to sway John.

12 CHAPTER

PRESENT DAY: A SECOND MEETING

It had been several weeks since my meeting with James Bull Wings, and now I was back in the comfortable 3rd floor living room again. During the first meeting he had asked me all sorts of questions about my family. He had asked to feel my face and commented that I had high cheek bones. He asked if this trait ran throughout my family and if we had Native American lineage in our family. Remarking that, "Every black family claims to have a little Indian in them," I told him that I was told that my mother's great grandmother was full-blood Cherokee, and that this was were some of us had gotten the trait, noting that my mother and one of my sisters had the trait, but that my other brothers and sisters didn't. I explained to him that our family was a spectrum, and that the seven of us brothers and sisters ranged from very dark to very light with curly hair, mentioning how I almost got into a fight because this one kid called me a liar when I told him we were brothers after he asked why we were dressed alike. *I have no idea why my mother always dressed us as if we were triplets.* Smiling, as we finished the discussion, he said that he would try to look further into my mother's family's history.

Today, as I sat across from Mr. Bull Wings, I asked, "So what crazy things have you found out about my family?"

"I still have a bit more research ahead of me and more people to talk to, and part of that research is getting more information about you and your family," He replied. "In particular, I'd like to know about various events in your or your family's life. Let's start with any stories that were passed down in your family."

Metamorfose

I told him about one of my brothers being born with a veil on his face, which supposedly meant that he could see things the rest of us couldn't. I told him about the story I heard about a pot of money that was buried in the backyard of our house in Petersburg, VA, that supposedly kept moving whenever someone in the family tried to get it. I told him about the stories I heard about the time when I was a baby, and my father thought he heard an intruder in our house, and how my mother calmed him by telling him that it was just her great grandmother's spirit making sure that we were safe. These stories use to fascinate me as a child but re-telling them now was kind of creeping me out.

James Bull Wings then asked me about any tragedies or near-death experiences in my family. I started with the story I heard about the time when my mother's father was a young man, before he married my mother's mother, and his legs began to swell to the point that he was bedridden and near death. I was told how her grandfather, Pop Fisher, put a silver dime on the bottom of each of his feet, and how the dimes turned black, which indicated that someone had put a hex on him; and how her grandfather proceeded to pour salt on her father's legs, and how his legs supposedly opened up as snakes ran out of them. I told him about the time when I was about four and a tornado had struck Petersburg destroying many houses but sparing ours. I told him about how we were all huddled together in the basement scared; noting that now that I thought about it, my great-grandfather, who I called granddad, seemed more determined than scared, and how my mother seemed fairly calm, maybe to calm us.

I went on to the time my friend Joseph and I went to play at a construction site, or really a demolition site; pointing out that at that time they didn't bother to put fences around construction sites in the inner-city. Forgetting his blindness yet again, I said, "If you look at any of the early Sesame Street shows, you'll see kids playing at inner-city work sites, running through huge pipes and things."

I continued, "The demolition site was where they were tearing down an old icehouse, the kind that used to sell

Metamorfose

those big blocks of ice. It was late July and it had rained
like 'cats and dogs' most of the week. When the rain
finally stopped, we were finally able to play outside, and
Joseph and I decided to go see what the rain had done
at the old icehouse site. When we got to the site, we
could see that the basement of the half-torn-down
building had filled up like a pond. There were big metal
containers, like the kind that hold heating oil, floating
on top of the construction pond. I can't remember who
came up with the idea, but we decided it would be fun
to jump from container to container. Joseph jumped
first, and I followed. When I jumped to the next to last
container it flipped, sending me into the water. As much
as I couldn't swim, I was more worried about the sharp
jagged pieces of steel that lay just beneath the surface.
As I went under the murky water, I felt as if I was
suspended in nothingness, neither sinking nor rising. It
seemed as if I was suspended there for a long time, and
I wondered how I was able to hold my breath that long.
I also wondered if it was true that a person's life flashes
before their eyes when they are drowning and felt
solace that no reruns of my life were yet playing. Then I
felt Joseph reach down and grabbed my hand. He

effortlessly pulled me out, and with a look as if nothing at all had just happened, he motioned with his head towards a staircase and said, 'let's go up them'. Assuming it was my fear and mind that slowed the time I spent in the water; I followed Joseph up the staircase. The staircase led to a door that opened to nothing because the other side of the building had already been demolished." I finished my summary of near-death experiences by telling Mr. Bull Wings about car accidents, and other seemingly normal incidents.

After I was done, I asked "How come you didn't question me about my spectrum of brothers and sisters?" Adding, "That's the one thing that I've always had questions about."

"I didn't bring it up but made a mental note to see if there is some type of connection to other things I uncover," he answered. "Once I've had the chance to meet with the rest of the people I've been trying to contact, and wrap up my research, I'll get back to you with everything I've found."

13 CHAPTER

THE 1950S: POP FISHER

There was a quick syncopated knocking at the door. It must have been close to midnight. It had been about three years since Pop Fisher had gotten a midnight knock with this distinct pattern. Without saying a word, he opened the door and hurried the knocker into the house. The knocker was a woman with a baby. He didn't ask her name, he had always found it best to sever all connections, and not knowing a name was the start.

The woman began, "I was told that this was a place where my son would be cared for and protected."

Metamorfose

Pop nodded his head in affirmation, thinking to himself, *"It's another boy."*

Pop didn't need, or even want, the backstory, all he needed was the special knock indicating the person doing the knocking was sent to him by someone he trusted. Pop took the baby and said, while showing the lady back out the door, "We'll p'tect em".

The Fisher family integrated these "door-nock" babies into the family. All the children grew up as brothers, sisters, cousins, aunts, and uncles, all believing they were blood relatives, and in some cases, they were actually blood-related although not as they thought.

14 CHAPTER

THE 1920S: THE SHAMANS

William "Pop" Fisher was the son of a Shaman who came from a family of Shamans. Unlike his forebearers and other members of the family, Pop didn't hold himself out to be a Shaman, but being one isn't something you choose. Want it or not, having access to, and influence in, the world of good and evil spirits is something that is with you from birth - before birth, and this gift was strong in Pop. Although Pop Fisher didn't do ceremonies and rituals, some people still came to him when they needed someone to intercede on their behalf.

Metamorfose

The first time that Pop and his wife took in a child was
when a couple came to Pop to have him intercede on
their daughter's behalf. Pop had interceded on the
husband's behalf when the husband was a young man
and gravely ill. His mother had explained that there was
a generational curse put on the family that would
manifest with the first born of their son's generation,
and that their son was indeed the first born of the
generation and was now very ill. Pop interceded and
healed the young man, and years later the man
returned with his wife and daughter asking Pop to
intercede for his daughter. During the intersession,
while in a trance like state, Pop saw the child's future
and told the parents that the only way to keep the child
safe was for them to leave her there. The couple was
distraught, but knowing that disobedience was what
caused the curse, they heeded Pop's words. While in
the trance, Pop not only had seen the child's future, but
saw his own family's future, and other children's
futures. A few years after the Fishers took on the first
child, a strange knock came on the door late one night.
It was a woman who told Pop that she was told that he

could protect her daughter. Pop accepted the girl

without question. Other children would follow, always

starting with a late-night syncopated knock at the door.

15 CHAPTER

THE 1800S: INFILTRATION

One day, following another contentious Council meeting, Bert asked Andrew to stop by his house the next day. When Andrew arrived at Bert's house there were several other people there with Bert, milling around the front porch. Andrew knew everyone there and waved a hello wave to the group. As Andrew made his way up the porch steps, Bert greeted him with, "Glad you could make it," then said to everyone else, "let's go inside."

Metamorfose

Bert's living room wasn't large but was big enough to comfortably accommodate the small group. As everyone settled on to a couch and chairs, Bert said "We will pick up where we left off last time."

Immediately Ray Suake began, "As I was saying last time, we can't keep waiting on John," his curly brown hair sweeping over his right eye as he instinctively turned his head to the left to look at Andrew as he said this. We are never going to get Jackson to honor the current treaty, heck, even Adams dragged his feet, and he was supposedly on our side," he added.

Looking around the room at the others, he asked, "How long do we continue to back John's plan?

Until the shooting starts?

Until our houses are on fire?"

Turning back to Andrew, Ray proclaimed, "If you can't get John to understand that we have now gone from the frying pan into the fire, and that the new treaty is our best option, then we'll have to act without him!"

"We've waited long enough," exclaimed Ben Baker, a gaunt man with a permanent look and demeanor of impatience.

"We have waited time and time again every time he has asked us to be patient, and now it's time to act," he said with spital flying from his mouth.

Others chimed in with 'that's rights' and 'yeahs'.

Shaking his head in acknowledgement, Andrew responded with, "I'm just as frustrated as you are, but we need to be united in our decision."

Bert finished up with, "Andrew, tell John that if the Council doesn't agree to sign the new treaty, we will act on our own."

Although they didn't want to outright say it in the meeting, the Treaty Party was already making plans to sign the treaty without the backing of the Cherokee Nation's governing body. Although the meeting appeared to be a last attempt to get John on board, Bert really didn't expect John to ever agree to the signing of a new treaty. What Bert really wanted was Andrew on his side. He felt having Andrew, *an Acquetakey* involved, would lend more credibility to the Treaty Party. Based on Andrews discussions, both in and out of Council meetings, Bert believed Andrew's sentiments had already moved away from John's thinking and closer to that of the Treaty Party.

16 CHAPTER

THE 1800S: THE REPORT MEETING

John, Joe, Adam, and Andrew were sitting at John's kitchen table. Andrew told the men, "They are talking about not waiting on the Council and acting on their own." Andrew described the atmosphere of impatience and anger that permeated the meeting, with Adam adding that the people he'd been speaking to were sounding more anxious and impatient as well. Stepping on Adam's words before he could finish the word "anxious," Joe responded incredulously, "Act on their own? They don't have the authority to act on their own!"

Metamorfose

"That's their threat," responded Andrew.

"We have got to shut them down now," Joe demanded.

They're not going to act on their own," John said, partially with a sound of authority and partially with the sound of determination.

Andrew said in a quiet pensive voice almost as if speaking aloud to himself, "What if they're right and this thing ends in a massacre?"

John responded, "The Government cannot just slaughter us! No matter who's President." With the sound of growing frustration with the whole thing John continued, "If the U.S. Government won't honor our current treaty, what makes anyone think they'll honor a new one?"

John ended the meeting on a calmer note, reemphasizing his belief that enforcement of the current treaty was best and asking Andrew to stall the

Treaty Party as long as he could, while John continued to work on pressing for compliance with the current treaty. He assured Joe that if Andrew's tactics didn't work, they'd take direct action against the "so called Treaty Party".

17 CHAPTER

THE 1800S: THE NEXT TREATY PARTY MEETING

Andrew was back at Bert's house for the next Treaty Party meeting. Bert got straight to business by asking Andrew how it went with John. Andrew lied and said that John was coming around but thought it would take more time for him to fully embrace signing a new treaty. He asked them to give him more time to work on John. Bert responded, "Enough is enough and we can't wait any longer." He informed Andrew that they had begun discussions with members of Jackson's Administration about signing a new treaty on behalf of the Cherokee Nation, without the Council.

Metamorfose

For Jackson, having the Treaty Party sign the new treaty would give him the veneer, of a negotiated agreement with the Cherokees, he needed to start the Indian relocation, and give those on the fence of the relocation fight a reason to have a clear conscious when the removal started.

There was a long silence in the room while everyone waited for Andrew's reaction. Although seething, Andrew kept is face calm, nodded his head, and said, "I understand."

Walking over to Andrew, Bert put his hand on his shoulder and asked, "Andrew, are you with us on this?"

"What's got to be done has got to be done," Andrew responded, then patted Bert's hand that was still resting on his shoulder.

Going all in, Bert said, "We'd like to also have you in on the meetings we are having with the Jackson people."

Metamorfose

"Count me in." Andrew responded, feigning enthusiasm.

As the meeting ended, each member that was there made sure to make their way over to Andrew to tell him how happy they were that he was with them. Andrew smiled, shook hands, patted backs, and exclaimed gladness too.

18 CHAPTER

PETERSBURG, VA 1965: NOT A KANGAROO COURT

The house was intact, but the family wouldn't be, at least not all together in Petersburg. Walking around looking at all the neighbors' houses that were barely standing or not standing at all, Pop Fisher murmured, "Lawd why s'much dev'station?" It seemed to me that grandad was blaming himself for the devastation, and I guess I also kind of felt guilty that our house was barely touched while my friends' houses were mostly gone.

The days that followed the tornado were ones of activity as everyone pulled together to help each other salvage what they could and clean up what they couldn't. The older folks and teens took on the harder jobs of up-righting vehicles, knocking down the rest of unsafe structures that were beyond repair, and fixing or rebuilding the structures that could be repaired. The younger children helped pick through things to find keepsakes and tried to organize the little bits of rubble into small piles that would, at some point, be removed. It seemed as if our family tried to work harder than anyone else to make amends for our house being spared, oftentimes starting at the break of dawn, and not stopping until it was too dark to continue working safely. We worked even longer once the electricity was restored to the streetlights.

It had been a couple of months since the tornado had struck, and although the neighborhood was nowhere near being rebuilt, the area looked better than it had looked right after the tornado. The visual progress didn't seem to lighten the mood in our house. Pop's spirit still seemed to be disquieted and his moods set the mood of the whole household. One day he gathered the family together in the living room for a family discussion. I never liked being called together for family

Metamorfose

discussions because they were normally for what grandad called his Kangaroo Court. When anyone of us, or in most cases several of us, did something wrong or broke one of grandad's rules, he'd call us all together and announce that he was holding Kangaroo Court, which meant he would be the judge, the jury, and the executioner for whatever offense we had committed. Many times, the punishment the executioner carried out involved a belt to the butt, a bar of soap in the mouth, or some form of hard labor, sometimes all three. I guess having us all there during his Kangaroo Court, the guilty and not guilty, was meant deter the not guilty from ever becoming the guilty. This time the meeting wasn't for holding a Kangaroo Court, but it carried all the seriousness of one. Once we were all there, grandad said, with a look of resoluteness, "It been 'cided that Gail and 'er fam'ly gonna go ta DC." I didn't understand why only some of us had to go to Washington DC, and I didn't want to leave my cousins. When I heard it was only going to be my parents and the five youngest kids moving, and that my oldest brother and sister were staying in Petersburg, I became inconsolable, burying my head into my father's chest I sobbed. He held me and in a comforting voice said,

"There are some things you will not understand now,

hopefully you will understand them later."

19 CHAPTER

THE 1800S: THE PLAN

It was just after 3:00pm and Andrew wanted to head straight to John's house after he left the Treaty Party meeting, but thought it was best to wait, in case they had not fully trusted him and had someone trail him. It was around 6:00pm, dinnertime, when Andrew came through John's open screen door.

John, his wife Anne, and their son John Jr. were seated at the dining room table, which was visible from the front door and vice versa.

John junior yelled, "Uncle Andrew is here!"

Metamorfose

Andrew walked the straight path through the living room to the dining room.

Anne asked, "Would you like some supper?"
Andrew replied, "No. I just need to talk to John."

The two men headed back to the front porch. Both of them half-set on the porch rail turned slightly towards each other, Andrew to the left of John with his right thigh sitting on the rail and his left foot fully planted on the porch floor, and John to the right of Andrew mirroring Andrew's position.

Speaking in a low serious tone, Andrew said, "John, they've started having discussions with members of Jackson's Administration about signing a new treaty on behalf of the Cherokee Nation, without the Council.

In is normal deliberative way John waited for Andrew to finish before reacting.

Metamorfose

Andrew continued, "They've asked me to join the meetings."

John asked, "What did you say?"

"I told them I'd be glad to," Andrew responded.

"How long have they been meeting with the Administration?" John asked.

"I don't know," said Andrew.

There was a long pause while John turned things over in his mind. Finally, he said, "Well it's good they've invited you to be part of the meetings. We better get with Joe and Adam tomorrow to let them know things have changed."

Joe was bursting with anger when he heard that the Treaty Party had been meeting with the Administration without the Councils knowledge.

"We have got to stop those fools," he exclaimed. "I'd rather die in a blood bath fighting those devils, than die piece by piece!"

Adam was in disbelief. Shaking his head he said, "I knew from my conversations with people that things were heating up, but I never thought the Treaty Party would follow through on their threat, at least not without making a final demand at a Council meeting."

John agreed, "Yeah, I thought they'd make a declaration at the Council meeting and officially split from the Council before doing anything else."

"Damn-it John, I told you we needed to shut them down," Joe said almost yelling.

With a defeated look in his eyes, John said, "you were right."

Adding whatever silver lining he could to the cloud of bad news, Andrew told Joe and Adam what he had told his brother, that they'd asked him to participate in the meetings with the Administration. He added, "This means they trust me to some extent, and I can monitor how things are progressing firsthand."

"How things are progressing?", Joe snapped, "they can't be allowed to progress at all!"

John added, "I can't agree more, it's time to act!"

With the weight of the fate of the Cherokee Nation on their shoulders, the four men came up with a plan to have Andrew try to sabotage the negotiation meetings. If that failed, they agreed, he would have to stop the signing of the new treaty by any means necessary. Andrew, weighing the gravity of the plans, assured them he would do everything in his power to not let the treaty be signed. In his mind he turned the words *by any means necessary* over and over again.

It was John and Andrew who would later define *by any means necessary* as a plan to kill the leaders of the Treaty Party.

20 CHAPTER

PRESENT DAY: A VISION FULFILLED

Although James Bull Wings' days had been mostly filled
with relaxing with his music, he still contributed to the
running of the store by using his years of experience to
offer advice every now and then to his children on the
authenticity of items they were acquiring for the store,
and by piping the music he loved into the store.
However, what really made Mr. Bull Wings' day were
those rare occasions when he was unfamiliar with an
item's possible origin and had to delve deep into
research about it.

Metamorfose

When a young man, who could have been the man he was supposed to find years ago, showed up at the family store mentioning the chance encounter the two of them had, and telling the story of a tri-faced Tornado and an unknown voice from his OnStar service that led him there, James Bull Wings reveled in the thought of helping the young man piece together his puzzle. *Their puzzle*!

He began by asking all sorts of questions about the man's family. After feeling the structure of the young man's face and noticing his high cheek bones he asked, "Are the high cheek bones a trait that run throughout your family?" Being told yes, he then asked, "Do you have Native American lineage in your family?" After the man described the Native American lineage that he thought ran through his mother's side of the family, Mr. Bull Wings said he would try to look into things further, focusing on the mother's family's history. Asking for the man's phone number, he promised to get back to him soon.

Metamorfose

For James Bull Wings, *looking into things* meant getting an understanding of the young man's family lore, and connecting it to other stories and hopefully written records. He would need to rely on his children for help with this and hoped they would indulge him. Looking into things also meant looking into his own family's background and exploring its lore since he was clearly part of the puzzle, how big a piece he didn't know.

21 CHAPTER

PRESENT DAY: LOOKING INTO THINGS

James Bull Wings began his research by trying to recall what history he already knew about the area that covered North Carolina and Virginia. To validate his knowledge and fill in any gaps, he and his children did further research on the area's demographics over the years, and other aspects of its history. To learn how the young man's family fit into that history, James Bull Wings had his children use Ancestry.com to try to get a fuller picture of the young man's family tree, and to review any records that were related to the names found on the mother's side of the tree.

Metamorfose

Searching through Ancestry.com was more tedious than expected, mainly owing to the poor nature of many of the source documents it used to create the database. The site mostly used old Census records, birth records, marriage certificates, death certificates, and military duty records to create its database and tease out possible connections that would facilitate the construct of family trees. Although they were generally a good source of historical information, when it came to African Americans and Native Americans, these documents came with deficiencies. The problem with the census records is that there would be variations of the spelling of names from one census to the next because census takers used to conduct in-person interviews. Often during the interviews, the census taker would write down whatever name they thought they heard or spell the names however they saw fit; this was particularly true when it came to them interviewing African Americans and Native Americans. For these groups, birth records were scarce, and when you did find some, the dates didn't always match with what was recorded in the other records. The site had other drawbacks also, for instance, there were times when wrong people were suggested by the site as being connected to a tree because their names were the same as someone who belong on the tree, causing the Bull Wing children to waste time reviewing records they didn't need to review.

Because of the infidelity and scarcity of the records for African Americans and Native Americans, the children also searched for state registries and any records that historical societies or lay historians had. It was a young lady from the Hampton Roads-Norfolk Historical Society that reaffirmed in James Bull Wings the need to know about things that weren't normally found in written records. When talking to her, she shared that although her real profession was accounting, she had gotten interested in Virginia history after hearing many fascinating stores from her classmates when she attended Old Dominion University. She said she would help put him in touch with the families of some of those classmates, especially the ones that came from the areas that he was researching. He, in the meanwhile, would meet with Marcus to find out about oral stories that were passed down through the family and to hear about various events that had occurred over the years.

22 CHAPTER

THE 1800S: ANY MEANS NECESSARY

The negotiation meetings Andrew attended were fraught with tension.

Andrew felt that Bert and his guys were letting themselves be bullied. To keep the wedge between the Administration and Bert wide, whenever Bert seemed to be ready to give in on a particular point, Andrew would coax Bert into holding his ground. He often cut Bert's reply's off and directly addressed the Administration with "We can't agree to that!"

Metamorfose

If not getting them directly off track, Andrew had at least succeeded in drawing out the negotiations.

Eventually the Administration dropped all pretense of the Treaty Party's ability to negotiate anything close to a fair new treaty, often issuing not-so-veiled warnings, and on a few occasions issuing direct threats. These warnings worried Andrew, but he kept replaying John's words in his head, *"The Government cannot just slaughter us, no matter who's President." The threats have to be just part of their negotiation tactics*, he kept reassuring himself as he continued to try to wreck the negotiations. However, he knew that the only way to truly know if someone was bluffing was to call that bluff, and that worried Andrew. If they weren't bluffing, his efforts to disrupt things could surely lead to the massacre the Treaty Party was trying to avoid.

Eventually, Andrew came to believe that the Treaty Party's aim of trying to stave off a massacre of their people outweighed having the Government comply with the original treaty, reasoning that even if Jackson agreed to honor it, he would do nothing to stop the states from breaching it. When Andrew, not only, did not stop the Treaty Party from signing the new treaty, but added his name to the document, he became a collaborator instead of an infiltrator, and in doing so, he betrayed his brother John.

When Andrew sent a letter to his brother informing him of his decision, John was furious. John had trusted his brother more than anyone else, that's why he sent him in favor of anyone else. John also knew that there would be a great price to pay for his brother's actions, not only for the Cherokee Nation, but also for the Acquetakey family. John had failed to choose the right person for the mission, and Andrew had failed to carry it out. Grasping the letter in his hand, John prayed to the Great Spirit, "forgive us for our disobediences, I promise we will make amends, we will make things right."

23 CHAPTER

THE LATE 1800S: ATONEMENT

When Emmy, Ben Baker's wife, noticed his horse near the house, midday, she knew something was wrong. Ben had always taken food for lunch with him when he went into the fields, not wanting to waste time riding back to the house to eat. "The quicker I'm able to do it, the quicker it's done," he would say, referring to any task he was doing in the fields on a particular day, whenever Emmy asked if he'd be coming back to the house to eat lunch.

Metamorfose

Emmy came out of the house expecting to ask Ben what was wrong, but he was nowhere to be found, so she headed to the fields to look for him.

There he was, at the edge of one of his fields, flat on his stomach. As her heart raced, her mind, in denial, thought *maybe he decided to nap*, knowing in the back of her mind that most people napped in a sitting position when they were outside. When she got closer, she could see that his head, twisted to the left, was arched up awkwardly as the right side of his face rested against a large stone. The permanent look of impatience on it erased by death's calm. Surely his neck was broken.

After Ben's funeral, people talked about what a shame it was that Ben at been thrown from his horse. People shared their own stories of being on their horse when it was spooked by a snake, stepped in a ditch, or caught a tree root with its hoof. They would compare scares or tell how they held on for dear life until they got the horse back under control. One told of his horse landing on him after tripping, "Almost crushed my leg!"

Metamorfose

Ben Baker's tragic death was still on everyone's mind when Ray Suake took his own life. As the word spread, people pieced together the scene. "Gun under the chin," someone had heard supposedly from someone who was there when they found him." "Gaping hole out the top of his head," another had said. "Brown hair, pieces of skull and brain all over the back porch," someone else heard. "His gun, a couple of feet from his hand." These two tragedies, less than six months apart added to the anxiety of the Cherokee Nation. There was a lot of discord after the Treaty Party's signed the new treaty. With people taking sides, the once united group now had two heads, and as one elder put it, "Anything with two heads is a demon." Friends and neighbors argued whether the new agreement was best for the tribe. They argued about the Treaty Party acting on the Nation's behalf without consent of the National Council. The anxiety led to arguments over just about everything, both large and small.

Bert was anxious too. He wondered if Ray's conscious had gotten to him. Seeing the Cherokee Nation splitting itself apart, even he was beginning to reconsider if going behind the Council's back was the right thing to do. When John told Bert he had a plan that would bring the Nation back together, Bert readily agreed to meet with him.

24 CHAPTER

PRESENT DAY: A VISION FULFILLED - BULL WINGS FOLLOW-UP MEETING

It had been several weeks since James Bull Wings had met the man, he thought he was destined to help. He, assisted by his children, was making decent progress on gathering information that would be the underpinning of that help. Now he was back in his living room gathering more information from Mr. Elstone.

"I still have a bit more research ahead of me and more people to talk to, and part of that research is getting more information about you and your family," he said.

Metamorfose

"In particular, I'd like to know about various events in your or your family's life. Let's start with any stories that were passed down in your family." After Mr. Elstone finished telling him several family stories that had fascinate him as a child, James Bull Wings asked, "Can you tell me about any tragedies or near-death experiences, big or small, that has happened in your family?" Mr. Bull Wings was riveted by the stories of snakes running out of someone's legs, a tornado skipping over Marcus' grandfather's house, and Marcus' surreal near drowning. Already trying to piece together in his mind how these stories and events fit with the information he had already collected; he also added a mental note to see if there was something more to the Elstone family and their array of children.

As he ended this second meeting, Mr. Bull Wings said, "Once I've had the chance to meet with the rest of the people I've been trying to contact, I'll get back to you with everything I've found."

25 CHAPTER

THE 1800S: BLOOD LAW

It felt like two lifetimes ago since Bert and John had considered themselves friends, or at least comrades. They were both serious-minded men who had found a bond over their desire to advance the causes of the Cherokee Nation, often finding themselves on the same side of an issue. When it came time to select the new leader of the Cherokee National Council, both men were considered strong candidates, and neither one of them cared who was selected as long as it was one of them. When the U.S. Government began breaking its treaty with the Cherokee Nation, both John and Bert advocated for forcing the Government to uphold their agreement. As discussions with the Adams administration dragged on, Bert began to become disillusioned. Later he would use the term *being a realist* as he made arguments for signing a new treaty with the prospects of holding the Government and Adams to their word and signatures. With every delay in enforcement of the treaty and every new infraction, Bert and John's viewpoints grew further apart, and by the time that Jackson was elected President it was hard to believe that these men had once been kindred spirits.

Now riding towards John's house, as he had done so often before their split, Bert's memories of their past collaborations fed his vision of him and John pulling the Cherokee Nation back together, even though he had yet to hear John's plan. He pictured them once again both addressing the Council, as co-protectors of the Nation, as kindred visionaries, as friends. Lost in his thoughts, Bert never really heard the report of the rifle, but felt the blistering hot pain in his neck, and then the warm blood pouring down his clothes as he fell from his horse. John rode up and dismounted near Bert. Gagging and gasping for air Bert reached for John with a plea for help in his eyes. When John took hold of his hand and said, "There's a price to be paid for betrayal of the Nation and we both know that price is death," the plea and all signs of life left Bert's eyes.

Making things right for John meant dispensing Blood Law. Under Blood Law if a member of the Cherokee Nation disposed of any lands belonging to the Nation without special permission from the Nation's authorities, the consequence would be death. Although there were efforts to replace Blood Law with the laws of the land, many people still abided by it.

26 CHAPTER

THE 1800S: BEN BAKER MEETS HIS MAKER

John had been planning for weeks, trailing, watching, and waiting. He decided that the best time and place to catch Ben would be early, while he was in his fields alone. This gave him the best chance of no one looking for Ben for hours.

As hoped for, John found Ben working in his far field early that morning. Ben was busy inspecting his crops and hoeing weeds. Ben was surprised to see someone riding toward him so early. He continued his work, glancing up every now and then to try to make out who the rider was as he approached. He was finally able to recognize John's face, and John's his.

John greeted him with, "Morning Ben."

 Standing fully up and resting his hoe over his right shoulder Ben replied, "Morning John. What brings you out my way this early?"

While dismounting John said, "Tribe business."

Ben, flabbergasted that John would come out here this early to argue, tried to cut it off with, "John, I don't have time for another argument, what's done is done."

With a calm voice John replied, "What has to be done is being done."

Ben contorted his face into one of confusion as he tried to decipher John's response, then into one of surprise when John suddenly pulled his gun from his holster and aimed it at him. Without thinking, Ben swung the hoe he'd been resting on his shoulder at John's gun hand.

Metamorfose

Before John could squeeze off a shot the hoe hit the gun, knocking it out of his hand. As John bent over scrambling for the gun Ben rushed him slipping the hoe handle over John's head, gripping the handle at both ends, pulling it tightly on his neck. John managed to slide his hands between the handle and both sides of his neck to try to free himself. While trying to push the handle away from his neck with all his might, John rolled his body to the left, throwing Ben off his feet, causing him to let go of the hoe. Again, John scrambled for the gun, but Ben scrambled too. The two men fought on the ground, swinging punches, and rolling over and over, trying not to let either end up on top. John's left hand clawed at a stone it brushed up against, and with a big swing he hit Ben on his right temple. Ben slumped on top of John. With labored breathing John rolled Ben's body off him. He rolled Ben's body over two times to get it near a larger stone. With the torso facing down, he grabbed Ben's head, turned it to the left and yanked up on it until he heard the neck crack. He then propped the right side of Ben's face against the large stone. He retrieved his gun, tried his best to remove any indication of a struggle, then mounted his horse and rode off.

27 CHAPTER

THE 1800S: STALKING RAY SUAKE

Luck or providence was on John's side when he killed Ben. Because of Ben's quick reaction with the hoe, instead of leaving him there with a bullet in him as planned, John left him there with a gash and a broken neck and staged it to look like an accident. He couldn't hope to be that lucky with Ray.

It took months, but John watched Ray the way he had watched Ben. Dusk was turning to night when John came around Ray's house, careful to make it seem that he had knocked on the front door first like any other

Metamorfose

visit, to where Ray sat on his back porch drinking. John had watched him for about an hour before circling around to approach from the front of the house.

Walking past the side of the house in the increasing darkness John yelled, "Ray are you back here?"

Sounding a little groggy but recognizing the voice Ray asked, "Is that you John?"

John replied, "Yes."

"On the porch," Ray said.

As he reached the top step of the porch, John said, "I'm sorry for stopping by unannounced, but this couldn't wait."

Before Ray could utter the question *"what can't wait,"* John was across the porch with his left arm tight around Ray's neck and his gun pressed under Ray's chin. John whispered through gritted teeth, "Good-bye traitor," and pulled the trigger. The bullet sent meat, bone, and hair blasting from the top of Ray's head. He searched the porch and then the house looking for Ray's gun. He found it in a holster hanging on a hook near the front door. He went back to the back porch, lifted Ray's head, and carefully positioned Ray's gun under his chin, matching the nozzle to the hole he'd just put there, and pulled the trigger. John, again, let the body fall then placed Ray's gun a few feet away from his hand.

28 CHAPTER

PRESENT DAY: NEWS FOR YOU

Sitting with my family on the couch in the family room watching "Frozen"- *still wondering how that song won an Oscar*- I feel my cellphone vibrate in my pocket. I check the number and realize that it's James Bull Wings. It had been four months since I had spoken to him. I move to my living room and say "Hello?"

In a tone somewhere between eager and anxious Mr. Bull Wings says, "We have got to talk!"

29 CHAPTER

THE 1800S: THE GREAT SPIRIT

John couldn't bring himself to exact Blood Law on Andrew, it would tear their family apart. Also, he blamed himself for Andrews actions the way he had always done ever since Andrew was a kid. He would leave Andrew's fate to the Great Spirit.

30 CHAPTER

PRESENT DAY: A PUZZLE NO MORE

James Bull Wings was astounded at the picture he formed once he pieced together, what he thought was more than likely, the correct pieces of the puzzle. He contacted Marcus, and with impatience in his voice said, "We've got to talk."

When I came to his house for the third time, I got there just as the store was just closing. Mr. Bull Wings' daughter Myra let me in the door and escorted me to the comfortable third floor living room. There, Mr. Bull Wings, and his son Jay, were waiting for me.

Metamorfose

As Myra showed me to a seat, her taking one also, James Bull Wings said, "I have a doozy of a story for you."

He added, "Keep in mind I had to fill any gaps in what I found by making what I considered to be reasonable assumptions based on the information I did have, and much of the information is from oral history."

Then he began, "Marcus, I believe you and your mother and maybe one of your sisters are not biologically part of the Fisher family," then paused for a reaction.

Although I had a *what the...!* look on my face, causing Jay to half-snicker, eager to hear everything I just said, "go on."

He continued, "From what I've gathered, along with their own children, the Fisher family took in many other children and integrated them into the family as brothers and sisters, cousins, grandchildren, etc. This made it difficult to unwind who might be really related to the

Metamorfose

Fishers and who isn't, and which of the children are related to each other somehow. I learned that the Fisher family are descended from a family that were Native American Shamans, and that they were often sought out to intervene on people's behalf with the spirit world. Your great-grandfather Pop Fisher, unlike his forebearers and other members of the family, didn't hold himself out to be a Shaman, but my understanding is that many people still came to him when they needed someone to intercede on their behalf. As the different versions of the lore, I've heard goes, your grandfather's reputation for his abilities to intercede grew and eventually led to people, whose spiritual situation called for more than intersession, to ask him to take their children to protect them from whatever curse there was on the child or its family."

Jay added, "And from what we have gathered, there's a real likelihood that your mother was one of those children, as well as some of your brothers and sisters.

As if this was a joint presentation, Myra, leaving out the qualifiers *likely* and *we believe,* said, "Not only was your mother one of what we've designated as the 'protected' kids, she, as did the other members of the Fisher house, also helped protect other kids by taking them to raise as her own.

"If we are not part of the Fisher family," I asked, "then who are we?"

Well, James Bull Wings said, "The history of your mother's great-grandmother being a full-blood Cherokee is true, but it's not totally accurate. While Pop Fisher's mother was also full-blood Cherokee, she is not your great-great-grandmother because as I said, you are not really part of the Fisher lineage. Everything I've found leads me to believe that your great-great-grandmother was the descendant of the Acquetakeys."

Of all the family stories I'd heard my whole life, "Acquetakey" was not a name that ever popped up.

"The Acquetakeys," he explained, "were prominent in the Cherokee Nation. John Acquetakey was one of the leaders of Cherokee National Council, and he had a brother named Andrew who worked along with him to help lead the Cherokee Nation through one of its worst periods in history." He continued, "When the United States began to renege on its treaty with the Cherokee Nation, John Acquetakey, as head of the Cherokee National Council started advocating for Cherokee resistance, and lobbying President John Quincy Adams, who was an Indian sovereignty supporter, to enforce the treaty. Things changed for the worst when gold was discovered in Georgia, and when Andrew Jackson, a supporter of Indian removal became President. After Jackson's election, a small group inside the Council broke with John's push for treaty enforcement, fearing that if they didn't sign a new treaty offered by Jackson, Jackson, having shown himself to be ruthless, would slaughter the Cherokee people. Although the terms of the new treaty only benefited the U.S. Government and had the Cherokee Nation giving up all rights to their land covering Georgia, Alabama, Tennessee, and North Carolina in exchange for land out West, the small group signed the treaty anyway, without the approval of the Cherokee National Council. This gave Jackson the veneer of a negotiated agreement with the Cherokees he needed to start the Indian relocation. It also gave people who were on the fence of the relocation fight a reason to have a clear conscious when the removal started. Signing the treaty ended up being a devastating blow to the Cherokee Nation and led to the Trail of Tears. It was also devastating to John Acquetakey because his brother Andrew abandoned John's efforts to force compliance with the original treaty and ended up joining the signers of the new treaty."

Continuing on, James Bull Wings said, "From the various versions of lore, in the chaos that followed the unauthorized signing of the new treaty, members of the Treaty Party, which was the name the small group had given themselves, began to die under what some thought were mysterious circumstances. Some stories attributed the deaths to the Great Spirit seeking retribution, while others said it was John exacting Blood Law on the traitors of the Cherokee People. One of the arguments I heard for it having to have been John is that Andrew Acquetakey was the only signer of the treaty that did not die. As the story goes, John couldn't bring himself to kill his own flesh and blood, which brought a curse upon Andrew's side of the family since he hadn't paid the price for betrayal of the Cherokee People."

I said, "Let me get this straight, I'm not part of the family I thought I was, instead I'm part of a family called the Acquetakeys that has a curse on part of the family."

"Your part of the family," Mr. Bull Wings said.

Handing me a set of hand-drawn charts, Jay said, "Based on the family tree we were able to piece together, it looks like you are descended from Andrew Acquetakey.

The first page of the charts he handed me started with John and Andrew's parents, then branched at the two sons, ending with their children. The second page started with Andrew's daughter Dilsey, branched at her children, then branched at her daughter Odessa, ending with her children. The next page started with Odessa's daughter Signora, branched at her children, then branched at her son Frank, ending with his children, one of which was named Gail.

"The story of how you ended up as part of the Fisher family is part of the story you told me about Pop Fisher healing your grandfather, as a young man, by pouring salt on his legs, which caused snakes to run out of them," James Bull Wings said.

He continued, "There are other accounts of this story; however, in those stories, it is said that a lady named Signora, who was Andrew Acquetakey's great-granddaughter brought her son Frank, your mother's real father, to Pop Fisher to have him intercede for and heal Frank, whose legs had swollen to three times their normal size. She told Pop she believed Frank's illness was part of the fulfillment of the supposed generational curse that was put on Andrew's side of the family, and that's why they came to him for intercession."

James Bull Wings continued, "When Frank got married and had a daughter, he feared that something would happen to her or eventually to one of her descendants,

Metamorfose

so in an effort to end the curse he took her, as his mother had done with him, to Pop Fisher for intercession. It was said that, during the intersession Pop Fisher saw the child's future and told the couple that the only way to keep the child and her descendants safe was for them to leave her there."

Jay, chimed in, "As you can see from the tree we developed, we believe that your mother Gail is the same Gail who was Franks daughter, which would make Signora her real grandmother, Andrew Acquetakey's granddaughter Odessa her real great-grandmother, and Frank your real grandfather, which matches your story."

"This is how your mother Gail ended up being raised by Pop Fisher's daughter Willie," Mr. Bull Wings said. Adding, "From what we were told, Pop Fisher and his family took in other children to try to protect them also, integrating them into his family.

Myra interjected, "That would explain the varied make up of your family. However, we couldn't determine why

Metamorfose

Pop integrated all of the children into his family instead of just being their guardian."

"Based on the stories we were told about why some of the other children were taken to Pop Fisher we believe there is a good chance that all of the children he took in were special cases like your mother, and that he must have had visions about their futures too," James Bull Wings said.

"Maybe the futures he saw were with them as part of his family, or maybe the visions were all connected, and it made it easier to protect them as one family", Jay offered. "Again, this is just our guess," he added.

"Whatever the reason, I believe having them all there as part of his family helped Pop Fisher protect them all, the way he protected everyone from the tornado you told me about" said James Bull Wings.

I sat there silently listening to what they were laying out, looking over the charts and timelines they had created, while trying to envision the whole story from beginning to end as if watching a movie in my mind.

After I had taken it all in, I said, "so how do us having to find each other fit into the picture?"

Mr. Bull Wings responded, "well we are part of the Muscogee Creek tribe, and although there were some skirmishes, our ancestors had a trading relationship with the Cherokee. Like the Cherokee, most of the Creek were forcibly moved off of their lands, which covered Tennessee, much of Alabama, western Georgia and parts of northern Florida, and were part of the Trail of Tears march to the West. So, we started racking our brains to try to remember stories that were passed down through our family and contacted older relatives that might be able to tell us about any direct contact our family may have had with the Cherokee. Of interest was a story about one of our ancestors, a great-great-great-grand father or something, who had saved a Cherokee's life during one of the intertribal skirmishes. As the story goes, the two men had become friends as the result of their longstanding trading relationship.

Metamorfose

Then one day parts of their tribes began warring with each other, and the man got stuck in Creek territory. It is said that his Creek friend risked his own life to hide him and sneak him out of the area. After the hostilities died down, the Cherokee, believing their friendship was preordained specifically for that moment of need, gifted the Creek one of the large sacred tribal drums his family used in intersession ceremonies, in recognition of the Creek being his guarding that day and interceding to save him. Although the story about how we got the drum and its importance was lost along the way, I am now pretty sure that the large drum that was passed down in my family is the same drum I have right now in my attic."

Jay added, "And if the Creek was indeed preordained to befriend the Cherokee to help him avoid a catastrophe, then, with a stretch of our imaginations, it's not hard to believe that maybe my father meeting you is a bit of history repeating itself."

"Knowing all of this now, I believe I was supposed to help you uncover your family history and help you figure out how to finally end the family curse," James Bull Wings said. He continued, "Remember what I told you about the words to the song that was playing in the store the first time we met?"

"Yes", I replied, "the song *Metamorphose*, you said that it was a song of repentance and that the lyrics translate into something like 'spare me oh Great Spirit and I will transform myself and do better' I believe."

"Yes, and I said that some people believed it originated with dying elders who were repenting for the wrongs or mistakes they had made in this life, and were petitioning to comeback as something better, while others believed it originated as a pact between a person and the Great Spirit because the person did something they shouldn't have done or didn't do something they should have done," he said. "While I have no idea what you specifically need to do to break the curse, I do know it has to start with you reconnecting with your real family and the Cherokee Nation."

31 CHAPTER

PRESENT DAY - FOUR YEARS LATER: REDEMPTION

My heart is pounding inside my chest. Three men are seated at a table with their backs to me, waiting for me to get there before the Government representatives arrived. This was the small group that wanted to sign an agreement with the U.S. Government, giving the Government the rights to oil reserves found on Cherokee Nation land in exchange for money and other promises. These were men I had come to know well, working beside them for two years to support their cause. It was my mission to stop them by any means necessary. *This is my chance,* I thought. W*hen you kill*

Metamorfose

the head, the body will perish.

John's side of the family was redeemed when he delivered on his mission to uphold "blood law" and assassinated the leaders of the Treaty Party. It was now redemption time for my side of the family.

I stood there for what felt like an eternity, shaking on the inside but steadying myself, contemplating the futures that would result from my actions today, and contemplating how history would portray me, hero, or villain. I breathed deeply and moved toward the men seated at the table, rubbing a sweaty palm across my thigh to the waistband of my pants. As I got close to the man seated in the middle, the baseline from "Metamorfose" thumping louder and faster in my head sounding like a large drum, I raised my semi-automatic and thought, *I will make it right; I am a better man than before*!

ABOUT THE AUTHOR

Gordon T. Alston was born in Petersburg, VA, the fifth of seven children. When he was one year old his parents David and Gilbertha Alston moved the family to Washington, DC where he was raised. After attending DC Public Schools, including H.D. Woodson Sr. High, he received a bachelor's degree from The University of the District of Columbia and a master's degree from Howard University. He is the author of two children's books, *1-2-3-4 Aidan Likes to Explore* and *Anika's Pickle Pie*. He currently resides in Columbia, MD with his wife Nicole and their two children Anika and Aidan.

The author's original sketch for the book cover.

OTHER BOOKS BY THE AUTHOR

Made in the USA
Middletown, DE
04 November 2023

41732208R00085